Written by David Bedford
Illustrated by Susie Poole

First published 2016 by Parragon Books, Ltd.
Copyright © 2018 Cottage Door Press, LLC
5005 Newport Drive, Rolling Meadows, Illinois 60008
All Rights Reserved

10 9 8 7 6 5 4 3 2

ISBN 978-1-68052-454-3

You're a **BIG** Sister

PaRragon.

You're going to be a big sister!
And that's so lucky for you ...

Babies LOVE their big sisters

and all the smart things that they do.

Big sisters know
babies like quiet,
so just smile
and whisper, "Hello."

Big sisters are really good helpers.
Let's all get ready ... and go!

All babies are cute ...

fun ...

and cuddly,

but there are things a big sister
soon knows ...

Babies dribble ...

kick ...

and might even be sick ...

all over your clothes
and your toes!

Though they are so very tiny,
babies can make a BIG STINK ...

And when they're not feeling well ...

babies scream ...

and yell ...

so loud you can't hear yourself think!

Babies haven't learned to play fair yet.
But remember, you were little once, too!

So be kind and share ...

Cuddle, play, and take care ...

And help them be
clever like you!

When Mommy and Daddy are busy,
always know that they love you, too ...

And now that you're a big sister,

enjoy sharing with
somebody new!